The spirit o

Henry Farrell

Alpha Editions

This edition published in 2024

ISBN : 9789361470912

Design and Setting By
Alpha Editions
www.alphaedis.com
Email - info@alphaedis.com

As per information held with us this book is in Public Domain.
This book is a reproduction of an important historical work. Alpha Editions uses the best technology to reproduce historical work in the same manner it was first published to preserve its original nature. Any marks or number seen are left intentionally to preserve its true form.

The SPIRIT of TOFFEE

By Charles F. Myers

Things were bad enough for Marc without having a friendly ghost messing up his life—but Toffee only made matters worse!...

In his private office the guiding light of the Pillsworth Advertising Agency sat behind his desk and looked slightly haunted.

And Marc Pillsworth was not the sort to look haunted without a good and sufficient reason. In this case, the reason seemed to be not only good and sufficient but rather spine-tingling into the bargain. Marc closed his eyes and made a real effort to suppress a nagging impulse to scream. But when he looked again the situation across the room had not noticeably bettered itself; the shoe was still in front of the chair, hanging indolently in mid-air.

In the last few minutes Marc had closed his eyes repeatedly, telling himself that the shoe was only a product of his imagination, an apparition born of a mind that had given way under an overwhelming burden of financial and domestic worries. But always, when he opened his eyes again, the shoe was still there, resting rakishly on nothing at all, seeming to stare at him evilly with its beady eyeletes. Also, there was something about the hateful thing that bespoke its owner's rather pungent personality. It had a look about it that was unmistakably aw-go-to-hell. It was a look that Marc found particularly distasteful, for it could mean only one thing. No getting away from it. George was back. And Marc wished he wasn't.

Marc had learned of George's existence through a previous experience so bitter it all but galled him just to think about it. When the ghost, Marc's own, to be explicit, had first descended to this region under the misapprehension that Marc had accidentally terminated his own earthly sojourn, he immediately impressed himself on everyone as a trouble maker of the first hot water. And, as though his strikingly original haunting activities hadn't been enough, he had resorted to random methods of mayhem in an effort to make Marc's demise an untidy actuality so that he, George, might thereby secure his own position as a permanent earthly "haunt." The affair had not been a picnic for Marc.

Though the wayward spectre, when materialized, was an exact duplicate of Marc in all physical respects, there the similarity did a screaming about face and streaked rapidly in the opposite direction. Where Marc was sober and serious-minded, George was a veritable connoisseur of all things viceful and frivolous. And where Marc was inherently honest, modest and retiring, George was frankly a crook, a braggart and rank exhibitionist. Also, it was not consoling that the spirit was extremely careless in the manipulation of his ectoplasm ... a thing that any other, right-minded ghost would go to any lengths not to be.

If Marc looked on the reappearance of George without pleasure, his attitude was not entirely unwarranted.

Marc glanced at the shoe again and shuddered. Absently he wondered how he would ever manage to explain the silly thing if someone should suddenly pop into the office unannounced. Obviously, something had to be done about it; he couldn't just let it go on dangling there, looking smug and complacent like that. And certainly it showed no inclination to leave of its own accord. In fact, it seemed quite content, as though it might just go on hanging around forever. Clearly, the situation demanded positive action. With quiet deliberation Marc lifted a bronze paper weight from his desk and aimed it with care.

The weight only grazed the toe of the shoe and fell dully to the carpet. But at least it produced some effect. The shoe instantly vanished. Marc leaned back and pressed a trembling hand to his eyes. Then he glanced quickly up through a haze of apprehension as a voice ... a duplicate of his own ... echoed across the room.

"Well, I'll be damned!" it exclaimed. "My ectoplasm must have slipped. How long has that shoe been showing?"

"Showing?" Marc said in a voice sounding a good deal less like his own than the other. "The awful thing has had me close to gurgling dementia for nearly ten minutes now. And if you must speak to me, please have the decent good grace to show yourself. It makes my spine fairly lurch to hear a voice coming out of nowhere like that."

Marc didn't realize the folly of his request until too late. Piecemeal, an arm, a leg, a mid-section at a time, George became visible, looking exactly like Marc right down to the last button.

Marc gazed on this phenomenon with utmost revulsion. "Can't you materialize all at the same time?" he asked fretfully. "Do you always have to come into my presence looking like the victim of a hatchet murder?"

George grinned agreeably. "Sorry," he said. "Can't concentrate on everything at once, you know."

"It seems you could at least concentrate on consecutive things," Marc grumbled. "You needn't break out like a rash." He looked up and blanched. Neckless, George's head was hovering over his collar like a loosely anchored balloon. "Oh, Lord!" he gasped. "How sordid!"

The head glanced around pleasantly, unaware of its airy isolation. It gazed admiringly down the length of the lean body beneath it. "Rather a nice job," it said proudly. "No foggy spots. Everything very flesh-and-bloody looking, I think."

"Bloody is right!" Marc croaked. "It all but drips with gore. For heaven sake complement that head with a neck before I scream."

George flushed prettily, closed his eyes and obliged. The missing neck sprang cooperatively into place. To Marc the spectacle was almost as repulsive as the disconnected head.

"Don't ever do that again," he breathed. "I'd never live through it."

"I'll try to be more careful in the future," George agreed.

Marc turned a quizzical eye on the ghost. He was being far too agreeable ... almost sickeningly so. In his face there was a sort of determined pleasantness that looked ill at ease in such unfamiliar surroundings. A suspicion stirred vaguely in the back of Marc's mind.

"If you think you're going to kill me with kindness, you back-stabber, just forget it. It won't work."

"How can you think such things?" George asked woundedly.

"It just came to me, all of a sudden, looking at your smirking face."

"You do me a terrible injustice," George replied. "You cut me to the quick."

"Believe me," Marc said relentlessly, "I'd make it deeper if I could."

"You're going to be ashamed you've spoken to me like this," George said. "I've come here to do you a favor."

"Then do me one. Go away. I've enough trouble as it is."

"Trouble?" George asked with sudden interest. "What kind of trouble?"

"Everything serious," Marc said. "Especially now that you're here."

George smiled thoughtfully. "Conditions seem about perfect for my mission," he murmured.

"Mission?" Marc looked on the spirit with open consternation.

"It's the High Council," George explained. "The big brass in the spirit world. They're making me do penance for the way I behaved the last time I was here." A shame-faced expression swept over his features. "They threw the book at me. They say I've set Spirit-Mortal relations back five hundred years and knocked their good neighbor policy into a cocked hat. Anyway, the upshot of the thing is that they've ordered me back here to haunt you until I've done you a good turn to make up for last time. And if I don't...." Here his voice broke with emotion and he shuddered. "They've only given me thirty-six hours to make good." He waved an unhappy hand at his materialized body. "And I can't stay like this too long, either. They only gave me an emergency issue of ectoplasm, so I have to use it sparingly." He looked at Marc pleadingly. "Though the idea thoroughly repels me, you've just got to let me do something nice for you. What can I do?"

"Off hand," Marc said unpleasantly, "I can think of any number of things for you to do. Without exception they are fatal and extremely messy."

"You don't like me very well, do you?"

"Since you force me to say it," Marc said flatly, "you disgust me. You disgust me through and through."

George glanced up, interested. "Through and through what?" he asked.

Marc's hand slapped hard against the desk. "Now, don't start that!" he grated. "This time, keep your simpering banalities to yourself."

"I only wanted to know...."

"Enough!"

"But if I'm going to do something nice for you," George continued doggedly, "I have to know what's troubling you, don't I? That's why I've been sitting around here half the night and all morning. Ever since midnight, I've been waiting right here for something to turn up that I could help you with."

Marc looked distressed. "Must you help me, George?" he pleaded. "Can't you just go on back to this Council thing of yours and tell them everything's all right. Tell them I love you like a brother. Lie your head off. You can do it. Only, please, please, don't try to help me."

George sank back in his chair with a sigh. "I couldn't do that," he said. "If I did, they'd...."

Suddenly he stopped speaking as a knock sounded on the door. He shot Marc an anxious glance.

"Dematerialize!" Marc hissed. "Disappear!"

George was instantly out of his chair, completely confused in his eagerness to do exactly as Marc wished. First a leg disappeared, then an arm, then his entire torso became foggy and vaporous. Suddenly the arm and leg reappeared again. He looked up at Marc, panic stricken, as the lower part of his face faded up to the nose, then stopped. He closed his eyes and seemed to concentrate with all his will. For a moment his entire body flickered like a weakening light bulb, disappeared, and promptly rematerialized in total.

"For Pete's sake!" Marc cried. "Do you have to keep flashing on and off like an electrical advertisement? Fade out, will you?"

The distress in George's face was genuine. He was earnestly doing everything he could to cooperate. "I'm too excited," he said. "Emotional disturbances always react on me this way."

The knock suddenly sounded on the door again, and Marc started as though he'd been struck. "Calm down!" he yelled. "For the love of heaven, be calm!"

George nodded, closed his eyes and breathed deeply several times. Slowly, a section at a time, he faded from sight.

Marc turned relievedly to the door. "Come in!" he called. Then turning back, he suddenly yelled, "No! Stay out!"

Like a great brown rat, George's shoe was loping lazily across the room. Apparently the spirit was habitually forgetful of this particular extremity. Marc raced after it and came abreast of it just as it reached the chair. He swung his foot behind him and kicked viciously. The shoe faded just in time to save itself, and Marc's foot collided painfully with the chair. Moaning, he sat down helplessly on the floor and began to nurse the offended member. Then, at the sound of Memphis' voice, he glanced up with horrified eyes. The secretary was observing him interestedly from the doorway.

"A new dance step?" she asked tonelessly.

"Just ... just getting a little exercise," Marc stammered lamely. "Got to tone up the old system once in a while, you know. Push-ups." He flexed his arms in half-hearted demonstration.

Memphis moved uncertainly into the room and closed the door. "Look out that chair doesn't push back," she said.

Marc laughed nervously and got to his feet. "I slipped," he said.

"Well," Memphis said resignedly, "since you've already cracked, I guess these can't hurt you too much." She extended a hand full of papers and dropped them on the desk. "Bills," she announced.

"The show?" Marc asked soberly.

Memphis nodded. "I dropped in at rehearsal last night, just out of morbid curiosity." She said it in a tone of voice generally reserved for use in funeral parlors and morgues. "I caught one of Julie's numbers." A look of utmost discomfort rested curiously on her ruddy face. "Sorry, Mr. Pillsworth."

Obviously Memphis was acting as the close friend who always consoles the bereaved.

Marc didn't know when the bug of theatrical ambition had begun to gnaw at the foundations of his home, but he was willing to bet an attractive sum that the craven little termite had been at its ravenous work for years, considering the matrimonial and financial devastation its insidious activities had wrought in just the last few weeks.

Julie's days as a model and "lady of the chorus" had dawned and waned long before Marc had ever met her. And that being the case, he was all too willing to forgive and forget them. Even in moments of domestic stress, when their handsome ghosts stalked arrogantly through his parlor, bedroom and bath, keeping Julie company as she proclaimed her intention to leave him and resume her "career" ... even then he refused to pay them any serious attention.

However, he might have displayed more wisdom had he given those days all the studied attention due a plan of atomic control, particularly during the last few months, during which, in Julie's reminiscences, they had taken on a more intense, misty-eyed glamour. But what Marc didn't know was that one of Julie's erstwhile chorus girl friends had recently arrived at a rather spectacular Broadway success.

For Julie, certain envious reactions had followed this event like a poison oak rash after an active day in the woods. The persistent weed of ambition that had been languishing in her innermost heart all these years suddenly flourished and blossomed forth like a tangle of deadly nightshade. From that moment on, though Marc was blissfully unaware of it at the time, the future of the Pillsworth marriage and bankroll was in deadly peril. Even Marc's better judgment was in jeopardy, for when it came to psychological warfare, Julie was just the girl to teach the War Department a trick or two that would probably curl its hair. It was no time at all before Marc was financing a fabulously expensive musical comedy, entitled "Love's Gone

Winging," and wondering what had ever possessed him. And all this on top of several outstandingly bad investments. The future was dusky indeed, if it still existed at all.

Marc stared unhappily at Memphis. "Pretty bad, huh?" he asked.

"If I told you what I think of your wife's talents, Mr. Pillsworth," Memphis said regretfully, "you'd either have to fight me or fire me. Maybe both. Mrs. Pillsworth may be a star tonight, but I bet she does a faster nose-dive than Halley's Comet. I hope she's getting a good rest today. She's going to need her strength."

Marc shook his head. "Got any idea what the total costs are so far?"

Memphis gazed unhappily out the window. "I'd rather not say," she murmured. "You'd think I was lying. I would, too. There just isn't that much money." Her gaze moved self-consciously from the window to the carpet. "The bank wants to see you right away," she added. "They were gentle but, oh, so firm."

Marc flinched. "I guess I'll have to see them," he said. "While I'm gone be a good secretary and make me a reservation in the nearest bread line."

"Don't give up the ship," Memphis said. "We can at least go down fighting. Even if it's only the creditors. In the meantime, business as usual. What do you want me to do about the Carmichael Aspirin Account?"

"I don't know," Marc said wearily. "See if they give free samples."

Memphis crossed to the door. "Well," she said with forced jauntiness, "I'll think of something. Maybe I'll just roll it up and fry it in deep fat." She slapped her girdle. "And I'm just the kid that could do it."

When she had gone, Marc turned forlornly to the window. He wasn't actually thinking of jumping, he was just wondering how long it would be before he did start thinking of it. Then he started as invisible hands began to pat industriously at the back of his coat.

"Stop that!" he yelled.

"I was only brushing you off," George's voice said, near at hand. "You got a little messed up on the floor."

"I'll dust myself," Marc said. "Thank you, just the same."

"I sure wish I could think of a way to straighten things out for you."

"Just forget it," Marc said. "Don't trouble your invisible little head about it."

"You need money," George mused. "That's the key to the whole problem as I see it."

"Sometimes," Marc said sarcastically, "you show signs of true genius."

George made strange musing noises for a moment. Then, unexpectedly, he asked, "Where's Toffee?"

Marc started visibly. He hadn't thought of Toffee in a long time, and he didn't particularly want to think of her now. One supernatural creature at a time was more than enough. Especially at a time like this.

Also, Marc was shudderingly mindful of Toffee's intimate relationship with pandemonium; the two of them romped about, hand in hand, like a pair of grade-school sweethearts. The most remarkable thing about Toffee, though, was that, in fact as well as fancy, she sprang from the very depths of Marc's own subconscious mind. Marc had long ago reconciled himself to the uneasy fact that his mind sheltered a precocious spirit who might, at almost any moment, be released into the world of actuality, and materialize right there before his astonished eyes. Then, too, there was Toffee's penchant for snatching the affairs of his life from his own grasp and instilling in them the breath of sheer madness. It was a difficult pill to swallow, and one that was rarely graced with a sugar coating. Even if she did manage to leave his life in a fair state of repair, her methods always put him through such a rigorous program of mental anguish that the end seemed hardly to justify the means at all. Marc tried to turn his thoughts away from her, for to think of her might easily start the chain of psychological reaction that always provoked her reappearance. He wished that George hadn't remembered the girl from his previous visit.

"I don't know where she is," he said. "Let's just try to forget her, shall we? Things are confused enough already. In the meantime, I've got to get down to the bank." He frowned thoughtfully. "But what am I going to do with you?"

"Oh, I'll come along!" George said eagerly. "There's no telling where I might stumble onto just the sort of thing I'm looking for. What's a bank?"

"They keep money in a bank," Marc said absently. Finally he shrugged. "I guess I'll just have to put you on your honor, though I've a feeling it's rather like putting a man-eating tiger on a lettuce diet. You'll have to promise to stay here and keep out of sight. I'll lock the office door so no one will walk in and surprise you. Do you promise?"

A perfunctory "uh-huh" echoed from George's direction. Then there was a brief scuffling sound and Marc's hat whirled crazily from the rack in the corner, flashed across the room and settled in a raffish angle on its owner's startled head. Invisible hands began to fuss at Marc's tie.

"Don't!" Marc cried. "How often do I have to tell you I don't want to be helped? Why can't you be yourself? I think I liked you better when you were trying to do me in."

"I want you to make a good impression," George explained.

Marc started toward the door. "That's very nice of you, I'm sure. But all I ask is that you just remember to behave yourself while I'm away."

"Oh, I will!" George's voice proclaimed earnestly. "I will!"

If Marc's mind hadn't been so filled with dread of the impending meeting at the bank he might have noticed that the voice was being just a little too earnest.

Marc turned the grey business coupe into a side street and headed for the parking lot behind the bank. He wasn't thinking too much, though, about what he was doing. Instead, his mind was occupied with a sneaking suspicion. There was something strange about the car, something odd about the feel of it and the way it rode. The body seemed to lean to the left a bit, almost as though someone were clinging to the side. Also, there had been the incident at the intersection, when a truck had broken through the light and headed directly toward the grey coupe. He could have sworn someone yelled at him to look out, someone very close to his left ear. It had given him a creepy feeling at the time. And thinking back on it, he was no longer so certain about the gust of wind that had brushed past him as he was closing the office door. It might have been....

Reaching the parking lot, he swung the car quickly to the right, into a drive, and pressed down on the gas as it turned onto a short, steep incline. Then he went tense in his seat. The post and chain barrier hadn't been visible from the street. Neither had the sign saying, "Use Other Entrance." And now that they were visible, there wasn't time to do anything about them. Sign, posts and chain were swarming over the car in a rush.

There was a tearing, whacking sound and the coupe jerked wickedly to the right. Suddenly, the steering wheel seemed to be leaving its post, spiraling upward toward Marc's face. A split second later everything went black to the raucous accompaniment of a blaring horn.

The horn continued to scream in the darkness, and, to Marc, its windy blast seemed to be hurling him outward. He shot swiftly out and up into lightless, unknown regions, his body curiously unhampered by the faintest trace of atmospheric resistance. He sailed through space, arms outspread, unrestrained, as though in a vacuum, and strangely, he felt wonderfully free, almost exultant. As he moved further into the distance the sound of the horn took on a thin, silvery tone that was almost musical.

Then, slowly, like a projectile approaching the apex of its arc, his body began to lose momentum. For a time there was the sensation of treading air as a swimmer treads water. Gradually, he churned to a complete, suspended stop. He felt himself hovering precariously in mid-air, and then, all of a sudden, he plunged downward.

In his descent there was no sense of easy motion as there had been before. Instead, he was falling rapidly, hurtling through the dark, a tangled mass of helpless arms and legs. His efforts to fight the force that was sucking him downward were useless. Then, sooner and more easily than he had expected, he came to rest. All at once there was a soft, cool surface beneath him that seemed to give with his weight, then lift him gently.

But his relief was shattered by a sudden, terrifying blast from the ghostly horn. Instantly, light began to show through the blackness which was being ripped into fleeting whisps and fragments by a strong, angry wind. Oddly, though, the wind didn't seem to affect Marc; it was blowing all about him without stirring so much as a hair on his head. He sat up and gazed at the scene before him as the last remnants of the shredded blackness disappeared into the distance. At once, the wind died and everything became quiet.

Marc was in the very center of a small grove of strange feathery trees that seemed to have deliberately arranged themselves into a perfect circle. A light blue mist lay motionless beneath the trees, blending softly into the green mossy carpet upon which he was resting. There was a cool restfulness about the place which he recognized at once. It was the feeling that always came to him when he entered the valley of his own mind.

He threw his hands out behind him on the grass and leaned back luxuriously. He was just closing his eyes when a soft sound whispered against the grass behind him. He started to swing about, but he was too slow. Mid-way, two cool hands pressed down gently over his eyes and two lips closed simultaneously over his mouth. The lips were not nearly so cool or so gentle as the hands, and they went directly to the business of kissing him with an air of abandon and authority. Marc struggled away from them.

"Guess who, you old monster," a voice whispered gaily.

"Unhand me, you perfidious little heller," Marc grated.

"Beast!"

The hands snapped away from Marc's eyes, and he looked up to see Toffee scowling down at him. Her green eyes were alive with annoyance, and her red hair hung loosely about her shoulders like cascading flame. Her transparent emerald-colored tunic was, as always, a completely disinterested party when it came to the matter of concealing her comely figure. One gold-sandaled foot was tapping a silent tattoo against the grass.

"Sometimes," she said evenly, "you turn my stomach. The way you keep shoving me away from you all the time, you'd think I wasn't gorgeous or something. It's beginning to ruin my self-confidence. Just a little peck or pat at the proper moment wouldn't hurt you any, you know."

"Do you have to be quite so effusive with your greetings?" Marc asked timidly. "Couldn't we just shake hands?"

"Shake hands!" Toffee exploded. "If that doesn't take the brass-lined girdle! I don't care what you shake. You can shimmy from one end of this valley to the other, but you needn't expect me to be a party to it. I wash my hands of you. And good riddance!"

And with that, she retreated to the far side of the grove and draped herself angrily against a tree, arms folded. She regarded Marc icily from the corner of her eye.

"Of all the thankless, gutless worms, I would have to wind up with you," she muttered. "You'd look good with your ugly head bashed in."

Marc flinched. "I'm sorry," he began cautiously. "I...."

Toffee was instantly in his arms, and he hadn't the faintest idea how she had gotten there.

"I knew you couldn't resist me," she cooed. "If you're really sorry...."

"Wait a minute!" Marc yelped, trying to free himself. "I didn't mean...."

The words froze on his lips. Over Toffee's slender shoulder he could see the blackness, whole again, rushing down on him, borne on the tide of the shrieking wind. His hands grew limp on Toffee's wrists as the darkness closed in swiftly and snuffed out the last glowing light of the quiet valley.

Then the wind caught them full force, and for a moment they swayed together under its sudden impact. Marc tried to get to his feet, but it was useless. Already, they were being lifted upward, shooting outward into space. Toffee's arms tightened around Marc's neck.

"Since you apologize," she whispered in his ear, "I forgive you."

Marc stirred and opened his eyes with an effort. Instantly, inside his head, a tin-pan symphony swung into a jangling rendition of "Hold That Tiger," and whaled it to a fare-thee-well. The universe seemed to rotate once, twice, and then skidded to a jittery stop and remained fixed. The discordant symphony became muted and distant. Marc discovered confusedly that he was in a sort of small shack-like structure. Bare boards with blinking knot holes stared back at him from an unlovely ceiling. Then an aged head blurred into sight, looking down at him with worried concern. It made a terrible clicking noise with its mouth and moved off to one side. Marc felt strengthless arms moving about his shoulders and with their negligible help, boosted himself into a sitting position. The owner of the head, a little, worried-looking man, was crouching beside him.

"You come around pretty fast," he wheezed. "Ain't really been out no time at all. You had me scared at first, though. Thought maybe you was hurt bad."

Marc stared out a slit-like door that was directly in front of him. Beyond, a row of assorted automobiles testified to his whereabouts. His memory jogged back a bit and arrived successfully at the accident in the drive.

"How's my car?" he asked.

"Not so bad," the man replied. "Bumper's ripped off, and the radiator's not so fancy as she used to be, but it still runs good. I drove it around here to the shack for you. Want me to call a doctor?"

Marc got shakily to his feet and awaited results. His nose throbbed dully, but the rest of him seemed all right. "Never mind," he said. "I'm okay."

"Guess the steering gear smacked you in the nose," the little man observed mildly. "Guess I shoulda put that sign down on the street. Sorry."

Marc nodded curtly and went outside. The grey coupe was standing alongside the shack, looking a little crestfallen with its twisted bumper draped loosely over one crinkled fender. He stared at it unhappily.

Then he stiffened.

There was a movement inside the car and a brief flash of red.

"It's on fire!" he yelled.

"I do believe," the sign-hider collaborated calmly. "Maybe we should look."

Marc ran to the car, the little man ambling casually along in his wake. Then they both stopped short as the red flash repeated itself at the window and was suddenly followed up with a puckish face. Toffee, her chin poised on the sill, peered out at Marc relievedly.

"I was wondering where you were," she said. "Thought maybe you'd been crumpled up on the floor. You really mashed things up, didn't you?"

"Oh, Lord!" Marc moaned. "Now I've got you on my hands!"

"It would be better," Toffee said insinuatingly, "if you had me in your arms."

At this point the little man shuffled over to Marc's side. "Well, I'll be!" he exclaimed. "I didn't see no woman in there before." He peered at Toffee nearsightedly, "You're one of them redheaded hussies, ain't you?"

"How did you know?" Toffee asked.

"Oughta know," the man said cryptically. "The old woman always blasphemin' about redheaded hussies."

"What does she say?" Toffee asked interestedly.

"Couldn't repeat it," the little man said, "even to a hussy."

"Then you can believe every word of it," Toffee said. And opening the door, she stepped lightly out of the car.

The little man gasped at Toffee's faintly obscured charms. "Oh, lady!" he sighed. "The old lady didn't say nothin' about anything like that!"

By this time, Marc was already at Toffee's side. He reached inside the car and quickly drew out a rather unkempt fur coat. It was one of Julie's old ones that she used for driving in cold weather. Fortunately, no one had remembered to remove it from the car. He threw it unceremoniously around Toffee's shoulders.

"It would make a refreshing change," he said darkly, "if you showed up just once without being in a state of indecent exposure."

"There are some," Toffee sneered, "who think this is one of the most decent exposures they've ever seen. And I'm inclined to agree with them."

Marc was in no mood to argue the point. He stared nervously at the inquisitive little man. "Let's get out of here," he said. "Accident or no accident I have to go to the bank."

As they left the little man behind and walked toward the sidewalk Marc poured out his troubles to Toffee. He told her of George's untimely reappearance and the unpleasant business at the bank. Mostly, though, he entered a stirring plea for her cooperation and good behavior. They had nearly reached the street when he suddenly stopped and raised a finger to his lips. A crunching noise sounded briefly on the gravel behind them, then stopped guiltily.

"What's that?" Toffee asked.

"Maybe nothing," Marc said. But he feared the worst.

Marc left Toffee just inside the bank entrance with firm instructions to remain where she was, to do nothing and say nothing until he returned. Also, he advised that she keep Julie's coat drawn tightly around her as certain misunderstandings were sure to arise if she did not. Toffee nodded and cooperated to the extent that she gave the appearance of a mute paralytic freezing in a snowstorm. The effect did not become her.

Upstairs, on the mezzanine, Marc made his way fearfully toward the president's office, a glass-fronted arrangement that overlooked the main floor of the bank like a guard tower in a concentration camp. As Marc approached, the president, looking up, caught sight of him and raced him to the door. The scene reminded Marc of a saber-toothed shark he had once observed in an aquarium, pursuing a small unidentified fish with murderous intent. Pausing for a moment, he glanced wistfully down at Toffee standing by the door.

Then he turned quickly and ran to the rail.

Even from that distance the mark of horror was plain on Toffee's face. Marc followed her stricken gaze and came very close to screaming.

Downstairs, in the clerk's enclosure, a riot seemed to have broken loose behind the counters. At first glance it seemed the clerks were merely rough-housing among themselves, but a second look told an entirely different story. It was a scene that flagrantly thumbed its nose in the face of credulity, spat on the carpet of comprehension and sashayed out the door of sanity with an airy flip of the hip.

The bank was thrown into a state of confusion as the money bags floated toward the door....

A pair of large money sacks, bearing the bank's name on their coarse sides, had plainly taken wing in a fit of convulsive madness. And whatever else these frightful sacks may have had on their minds, it was certain they possessed a boundless hatred for bank clerks. Progressing from the door leading into the vaults, they were savagely bludgeoning their way through the windowed enclosure, leaving a litter of prostrate figures and wilted white collars in their wake. The fugitive bags were making it emphatically clear that they would brook no nonsense from any faction desiring to frustrate them in their desire to be away from there. The current clientele of the bank was hastily arranging itself against the opposite wall.

One of the clerks, having miraculously escaped the ravages of battle, was streaking up the stairs to the mezzanine in a state of gibbering hysteria. Reaching Marc and the president who was now gasping at Marc's side, the fellow slowed to a sliding stop and began visibly to wilt with terror. The president grabbed him quickly beneath the arms and held him away from the floor.

"What is it?" he yelled. "What's going on down there? Tell me!"

The clerk shivered in his employer's arms. "I ... I don't know," he gasped. "I ... I was down in the vaults ... in the vaults ... making up the payroll for the Reedley Chemical Works ... and ... and...." His voice trailed off into a shuddering whine. "It was aw-w-w-ful!"

The president shook him energetically. "What happened?" he demanded. "Speak up, you ninny!"

The clerk's eyes rolled loosely in their sockets, fell inadvertently on the scene below and darted away. "Those two sacks of money ... they were behind me ... they went crazy all of a sudden. They flew up into the air and started singing and carrying on something terrible! Then ... then, they started out the door ... well, I tried to stop them. At first I tried being nice about it ... I tried to reason with them ... and ... and they *struck* me! And that isn't all! Those are the most foul-mouthed money bags in existence!"

The bank president promptly dropped the clerk to the floor. "The fellow's hysterical," he said. "It's a plot, a foul plot to rob this bank! Where are the police?" He stared over the rail and his question was promptly answered. The bank police, two of them, were trembling outside the enclosure, trying to nudge each other forward. "They practice the rhumba," he screamed, "while the bank is looted!"

At this point Marc left the president abruptly, vaulted over the collapsible clerk and made his way to the stairs. Half way down the flight he paused and prepared to take the second half in one heroic leap. There was no question in his mind that his suspicion had borne the deadly fruit he had feared; George had indeed followed him to the bank. Now the soulless shade, in a burst of misguided boy-scoutishness, was blithely playing fast and loose with the Reedley Chemical Works' payroll.

Marc made his appearance on the scene of strife in a confused sprawl that was far from heroic. Then, he sat up, bewilderment written into every line of his face. Not until this moment had he stopped to consider the course that he was about to take. Clearly, to be seen in close association with those demented sacks would be to invite disaster. The implication would be entirely clear to everyone, especially to the irate bank president. The only safe procedure, then, was to stay clear of the whole affair and let the money bags shift for themselves, which they seemed to be doing with remarkable agility from the sound of things behind the enclosure. Then he started with shock as a hand fell to his shoulder. He glanced up to find Toffee standing beside him.

"Don't do that!" he fairly screamed. "Don't scare me like that!"

"I don't blame you for being jumpy," Toffee said. "At the moment I could easily vault a twelve story building by sheer nerve power. That's the most soul-shattering thing I've ever witnessed."

"Help me up," Marc begged. He extended a hand toward Toffee, then promptly leaped to his feet, unaided.

Victorious at last, the dashing bags suddenly emerged around the end of the clerk's enclosure and sailed through the hinged barrier like a pair of high-spirited, slightly drunken seagulls. At the sight of them, the two policemen, who had finally managed to disengage their guns from their holsters, suddenly turned on each other in panic.

"Do something," one of them hissed. "Call a cop ... I mean, yell at 'em to stop. Say halt or you'll shoot. That's always good."

The other fidgeted self-consciously. "I'd feel silly," he demurred. "You yell at 'em."

"I'd feel silly, too," the other admitted grudgingly. "Silly as hell." He gave the matter his thoughtful attention. "Tell you what," he said finally. "Let's just turn the other way and make out we don't see. It's nothing no human eyes should be gazing at anyway. It's indecent to say the least."

Simultaneously, the cops turned their broad backs on the fearful spectacle and pretended to engage each other in casual conversation. "Tell me," one of them was heard to say in a strained voice, "and how is that charming wife of yours? And those two darling children?"

This chatty arrangement, however, was not destined to endure. The president's voice rang down from the mezzanine with such a volley of scalding invective and personal criticism that the two reluctant officers decided it would be the lesser evil to face their duty and do it, even if their souls fried in hell as the result.

By now the flying bags had singled out Marc and Toffee and were headed toward them in an affectionate rush.

"Go way!" Marc yelled desperately. "Beat it!"

But the bags were not to be put off so easily. They continued forward, dancing through the air in a sort of bottom-heavy samba.

"Let's take steps!" Toffee cried. "Lots and fast! Let's get the hell out of here before those fiendish bags put the finger on us!"

Physically, mentally and spiritually, Marc was in complete and utter accord with Toffee's suggestion. His whole being longed to its very depths to be away from those awful bags and the tailor-made life of crime that George so obviously meant to force upon him. Taking Toffee's arm he took as few steps as possible to the main entrance and swung the door open. Behind, the bags hesitated, seeming somewhat taken aback at this unfriendly gesture, then with a sort of shrug, started out in playful pursuit. The two policemen, their duties now engraved on their sluggish minds in letters of flame, joined the chase reluctantly.

Marc and Toffee headed instinctively toward the parking lot behind the bank, set on giving themselves every possible mechanical advantage in this mad race for respectability. Behind them, the bags steadily lost ground right from the start, probably because their weight held back their ghostly means of locomotion. Still further back, the two policemen, plugging along in their own flat-footed way, were hardly in the running at all.

Marc and Toffee reached the grey coupe at about the same instant and threw themselves on it like a couple of drowning sailors who had just sighted a lifeboat. In the midst of their frenzied activities the wizened attendant appeared at the door of the shack and watched with quiet interest.

"Wildest pair of young folks I ever seen," he murmured. "Leapin' around all over the place like they was crazy in the head or somethin'. Nervous type I guess."

Unmindful of the attendant's concern over their hurried activities, Marc touched the starter and put the car into rapid motion. There was a sharp hiss as the tires spit gravel into the air, and a second later a loud clatter announced the abandonment of the wrecked bumper.

But with the rapid exit of the grey coupe and its harried occupants, the little attendant's worries were destined to increase rather than diminish. No sooner did the car disappear down the drive than two bags, alarmingly on their own, flashed onto the scene and presented themselves before him in mid-air.

The little man looked at them, rubbed his eyes and looked again. For a long, tense moment he continued to stare at them. Then he turned about and stepped abruptly inside the shack, closing the door firmly behind him. He lowered himself into an ancient rocking chair, sighed deeply and closed his eyes.

"Keep a grip on yourself, you old fool," he muttered. "Sun spots ain't nothin' to get excited about. What if they do have People's Trust printed on 'em?"

The little man's grip on himself, however, might have slipped considerably had he remained outside to witness the subsequent movements of the "sun spots." Racing to a green sedan, they threw the door open and disappeared inside. A moment later the car, with no apparent aid, leaped from its place in line, grazed the fender of its neighbor, and went rolling swiftly down the drive.

As it was, two other grips were rudely pried loose by the incident. The two policemen, standing on the sidewalk, watched with horror-glazed eyes as the driverless sedan darted playfully toward them, then bounded over the curb and started in spirited pursuit of the grey coupe. To the one nearest the diabolical car this was not only the last straw, but the whole final load of hay. He turned disillusioned eyes on his companion.

"That's done it," he said in a hollow voice. "After fifteen years on the Force I'm going down to headquarters and fling this badge of mine smack in the Chief's homely mush."

"You can't do that," his partner protested, fingering his own badge. "You'd be quitting in the face of duty."

"If that's the face of duty," the saddened law enforcer replied, "then it had better be lifted before it gets any worse. I'd rather be buddies with Frankenstein."

"We gotta at least make an effort," his friend reasoned. "After all, them sacks ain't armed. And maybe there'll be a reward for their capture."

This last thought seemed to put a fairer complexion on the face of duty. The two trudged to the center of the street and hailed a passing taxi.

"Follow that car," the more enterprising of the two growled, directing the driver's attention to the careening sedan three blocks distant. "And if you catch it, I'll have you stored in the pokey for the rest of your life."

In the grey coupe Marc was driving with a suicidal brilliance such as he had never before displayed. Some sainted sixth sense took him safely in and out and around cars at times when it seemed that sudden death would surely be the result. All the while, Toffee busied himself with the diverting task of observing and reporting the progress of their pursuers from the rear window. The green sedan appeared to be doing dishearteningly well, probably because of its driver's hair-raising disregard for any and all traffic laws. George, with a splendid lack of prejudice, was using both sides of the street indiscriminately. On the other hand, the taxi wasn't faring nearly so well. Actually, it didn't seem to be really trying. According to Toffee's lights, it showed a distressing, sissy tendency to play strictly according to the rules.

Probably the only thing that prevented this lunatic chase from strewing the streets with death and tragedy was its early and untimely end. Allowed to continue to its ultimate conclusion, unrestrained, heaven only knows what madness might have ensued. The beginning of the end came swiftly when Marc cut the coupe screamingly through an alley and onto a side street.

Emerging from the alley, full speed ahead, he suddenly rocked the car to a jouncing stop that sent Toffee flying into his lap. Ahead and behind, the street was jammed to its curbs with automobiles of all descriptions, their horns bewailing their predicament in no uncertain terms. It was the worst traffic jam Marc had ever seen, and by some miraculous maneuver that even he, himself, couldn't believe, he had managed to wedge the grey coupe very nearly into its center.

From Marc's lap, Toffee reached slender arms toward his neck. "You impetuous boy," she giggled. "We love in the midst of danger."

Marc shoved her rudely back onto the seat. "We'll languish in the midst of Sing Sing, if we don't look out," he growled. "Where is that green sedan?"

Toffee peered out the window. "Good grief!" she cried. "It just pulled up in the alley. It's so close I could hit it with a pebble."

"Hit it with a bomb." Marc moved to Toffee's side just in time to witness the arrival of the cop-laden taxi behind the green sedan. The sight of the policemen was not reassuring; and neither was the sudden appearance of the money bags, darting stealthily toward them from the door of the sedan.

"Trapped!" Marc groaned. "What'll we do?"

Of course, the only answer was flight. Opening the car door, Toffee tugged at Marc's sleeve. "Come on," she urged.

"Where to?" Marc asked hopelessly. "We're jammed in here tight. Bumper to bumper and fender to fender, so to speak."

"Sounds lecherous," Toffee murmured. "Come on."

Marc was willing to be led, it appeared, even when he didn't know where he was being led to. He didn't object even when Toffee blithely opened the rear door of the next car, nodded cheerfully to its startled owner, and bounded through to the other side. In fact, he heartily endorsed the idea by rapidly following suit.

And Marc was not the only one to realize the wisdom in Toffee's methods. Soon, not only the pursued, but the pursuers as well, were romping in and out of strange vehicles with a reckless abandon that indicated a decided taste for the sport. The sound of wailing horns slowly died to be replaced by excited screams and dark curses. Toffee, easily the most fleet of foot, took a fast lead, Marc bringing up a close second. The skittering money bags, an early entry in this car-hopping sweepstakes, followed hot on the trail, flitting felicitously past the noses of astonished motorists like a pair of featureless rag dolls suddenly come to life. The two policemen, definitely dark horses without a prayer, brought up a couple of blue serge rears that lent a certain full-bodied homeliness to the affair. The reactions of the jammed-in motorists were varied and extreme.

One dapper little gentleman, the proprietor of a low black sedan, watched with bemusement as Toffee leaped lightly into his presence and made for the next car with business-like directness. But when Marc lunged after the lithesome redhead, the little fellow began to take an active interest in the proceedings, which, as he saw them, were becoming rather sordid. He held an arresting hand up to Marc.

"Why don't you let her go, mister?" he asked reprovingly. "You're running the poor kid nearly ragged. Maybe she just doesn't like you."

Marc brushed the hand impatiently aside and continued on his way.

The little man squared his shoulders manfully, slid across the seat and hopped quickly out the door.

"Maybe it isn't any of my business," he muttered, jumping to the running board of the next car, "but somebody's got to be there to protect that poor child when he catches her!"

The little man had no way of knowing that he was setting a dangerous precedent. Flinging one's self in and out of strange automobiles seemed to be just the sport that all America had been waiting for. Within only a few minutes after the beginning of the chase, the number of participants had increased by leaps, bounds and broad jumps. Clearly, there was an irresistible appeal about the thing that captured the imagination. With a why-didn't-I-ever-think-of-this gleam in their eyes people were soon leaping from car to car like a horde of salmon shooting the rapids at spawning time.

There was, however, a dreary minority in the traffic jam that found certain aspects of this frolicsome pastime highly objectionable. One of this number, particularly, was Mrs. Priscilla Carthwright, a matron of some standing who hadn't been known as "Prissy" during her girlhood for nothing. Mrs. Carthwright suffered an unconditional defeat, however, in her efforts to defend the sacred confines of her limousine from the ravages of the joyous herd. Crouched on ample knees on the seat of the car, she came dangerously close to falling into a swoon as the door burst open under her protesting, bejeweled hand, and a lank young man burst unconcernedly into her august presence with a broad wink and a primitive whoop that was strongly reminiscent of the cries of avenging Indians in the days of the early West. In the end, though, drawing on the waning reserves of her courage, Mrs. Carthwright managed to waylay one lean bespectacled reveler long enough to score her own little moral triumph.

"What does all this mean, young man?" she demanded imperiously. "Just where do all these people think they are going?"

The young man paused long enough to take the question under thoughtful consideration, obviously a matter that had heretofore not troubled him. "I think we're marching on Washington," he murmured finally, "to demand our rights."

"Just as I thought!" Mrs. Carthwright boomed triumphantly, dismissing her victim. "Communists!"

And having said, she settled back in the seat, cross-legged, her features fixed in a glassy stare that suggested haughty royalty in exile.

And there were other unfortunate incidents. Particularly bad was the one in which Toffee, completely innocent of purpose, threw the door open on a young couple locked in an amorous embrace. The lovers, looking up to find themselves observed by what appeared to be a surging sea of prying eyes, came close to sharing an hysterical fit. The young lady, in a seizure of confused madness, turned on her adored one and dealt him such a stinging blow in the mouth that several of his front teeth were completely dislodged. Clearly, it was the death blow to a beautiful, if careless, romance.

More gratifying was Toffee's foray into a bus load of energetic young basketball players. Though the delighted redhead was relayed from seat to seat and finally lifted out of a rear window with all dispatch, when she waved good-by to her instantly-won admirers, she was wearing a crimson sweat shirt with a golden N splashed across its front. Also, she had been unanimously elected the team's mascot in favor of an infant pig.

And so the racing procession continued, unabated, in limousine and out sedan, over jeep and under truck, for the better part of a quarter of an hour. And it might have continued longer had it not been for the enterprising spirit of a nearby restauranteer who rolled several kegs of beer onto the sidewalk thereby introducing into the occasion a further distraction. And since spontaneous entertainment is invariably the best, the wandering motorists were not long in realizing the inherent possibilities in this delightful turn of events. Other divertissments, including street dancing and a sidewalk performance by a theatrical troupe from a neighborhood burlesque, were quickly added to the program.

Never in the history of the city had the police been confronted by such an ungovernable, pleasure-bent traffic jam. After several futile attempts at laying down the fun-loving uprising, the Chief of Police and his aides finally accepted the inevitable, roped the area off from further traffic, and went in search of a cooling tumbler of beer. The Chief, sitting democratically on the curb, bending his elbow with refreshing regularity, was a little worried, however. He wasn't at all sure how the Mayor was going to look on this incident, and tomorrow there would be the tiresome business of restoring abandoned vehicles to their subdued owners. For his own part, he didn't feel there was any harm in the thing. Here was a group of jaded, work-weary city dwellers having their first delightful taste of real, communal fun in a long time. After his fifth mug of beer, though, the Chief's worries began to vanish. He decided he didn't really give a damn what the Mayor thought.

Toffee and Marc, however, were not among those participating in these impromptu sidewalk festivities. They had resigned their charter membership in the reveling brotherhood some time before the beer rolled onto the scene.

Stylishly garbed in a fur coat and the flaming red jersey, which came nearly to her knees, Toffee burst onto the sidewalk from the door of a glittering convertible, looking a little like a grand dame who had recently suffered some extremely devastating losses in a cloak room crap game. Her face a bit flushed from her recent triumphs, she turned and waited expectantly for Marc. Soon, her vigil was rewarded. Marc, hatless, tieless, his hair hanging loosely in his eyes, staggered through the convertible and moved breathlessly to her side. His eyes were immediately drawn to the garish sweat shirt.

"Where on earth did you pick that up?" he asked with distaste.

"A charming group of youngsters gave it to me," Toffee told him proudly. "Also, they favored me with several choice bruises." She ran a hand gently over her thigh. "Those kids sure know their way around."

Marc wasn't really interested in the precociousness of the younger generation. Not at a time like this. He glanced nervously over his shoulder. "Have you seen those ghoulish bags lately?"

Toffee shook her head. "I think we've given them the slip. The cops, too. The last time I saw those two flatheaded flatfoots they were slobbering all over each other like a couple of rejected brides. I really think they've lost their reason. One of them was mumbling something about hurling the Chief into the Mayor's face, whatever that means."

"Now what do we do?" Marc asked. "We're free, but we haven't a car any more."

Toffee crooked a slender finger. "Follow me," she said. "There is madness in this method. But it'll still work."

She led Marc around the block, back to the alley that had proved their one-way path to dilemma in the first place.

Marc hung back. "What's the idea?" he asked.

"The taxi," Toffee explained brightly. "The one the cops arrived in. It's the only transportation for miles that isn't all tied up. And it's just waiting for someone to come along and snag it."

Marc shrugged wearily and followed without protest as Toffee crossed to the driver's window and stuck her head inside.

"Is this car for hire?" she smiled.

The driver, an open-faced fellow of obvious good will, smiled back. "I'm supposed to be waitin' here for a couple of cops, lady," he said. "They said I wasn't to leave till they told me. They said...." Suddenly he broke off, his eyes focused on Toffee's fiery red jersey. "Say! Ain't that one of Neopolitain High's sweat shirts you got on there?" Admiration grew in his face as Toffee nodded. "I gotta kid over at that school, lady. I bet you have too." Toffee maintained a discreet silence on this point. "Maybe you seen my kid play basketball sometime."

Toffee looked at the driver closely. "Is he a tow-headed little devil with searching blue eyes?" she asked.

"Could be, lady. Sounds like him. He's a real nice kid."

Toffee's answering laugh was brief and bitter, but the driver didn't notice. He was busy opening the rear door.

"Hop in!" he said grandly. "Anything for good old Neopolitain High!"

Climbing into the cab, Toffee rubbed her thigh reflectively. "Yeah," she murmured. "Anything."

Marc and Toffee collaborated on a deep, heart-felt sigh of relief as the taxi backed out of the alley and onto the street. They didn't know, however, that the breath they were expending with such satisfaction was soon to be reclaimed in a horrified gasp. This curious phenomenon occurred only a moment later when the taxi slowed to a stop at the corner signal.

They didn't see the sacks approaching; the fearful things were just there at their feet all of a sudden, having arrived with a sickening plop. The car door on Toffee's side swung open, and there was suddenly another depression in the seat. The door closed again just as the taxi pulled out toward the intersection. Apparently the driver hadn't noticed.

"Thought I'd never catch up with you two," George's voice said breathlessly and pleasantly. "It was all a lot of fun, of course, but a bit fatiguing, don't you think?"

With a soul-searing groan Marc closed his eyes and sank deeper into the seat.

"Go strangle yourself," Toffee suggested waspishly.

But George's high spirits would not be quashed. "I really fixed things up, didn't I?" he asked proudly. The money bags leaped from the floor and deposited themselves in Marc's shrinking lap. "How's that, old man?"

Marc responded to this inquiry with a brief strangling noise. His face was turning crimson.

"What's the matter with him?" George asked. "Something disagree with him?"

"I think it's money poisoning," Toffee said dully.

"Well," George sighed, "now that I've set things right, I guess I might as well just relax and enjoy myself from now on. It's only four o'clock. That leaves me sixteen whole hours just to have fun. Until tomorrow noon. All's well that ends well, eh?"

Marc said a very singular and unprintable thing.

The driver turned and regarded Marc interestedly. "How come?" he asked. "You been blabbin' your head off and that's the first time you moved your lips. I been watchin' in the mirror. You a ventriloquist?"

"Yes," Toffee answered for Marc. "He throws his voice like crazy."

Apparently, the driver was not the sort to ask too many questions. He accepted the fact of Marc's voice tossing accomplishments on Toffee's say-so. And his attitude toward his customers instantly warmed. Confiding rather bashfully that he'd always thought of his own singing voice as something rather special, he burst into an unsolicited rendition of "Mexicali Rose" that had his helpless audience cringing in their seats. A truly ghastly moan issued from George's vicinity.

And it was a moan that Marc would certainly have echoed had he been able. He was wondering if a sort of plague of theatrical ambition had descended on all humanity. Thoughts of Julie and the imminent opening of "Love's Gone Winging" crept despairingly through his mind. He tried to console himself with the old bromide that things were always darkest before the dawn, but he couldn't help wondering where fate had stumbled onto this newer, darker shade of black and why the nights of misfortune had to be so interminably Alaskan.

Afterwards, it seemed to Marc that it was Toffee who suggested that they hide themselves in a movie theater. It seemed so, but Toffee stoutly denied it. But Marc's memory of that dark period was far too confused to be relied upon. Certainly, though, it was Toffee who invited the taxi driver along so that they might hide the money bags under the seat of the cab.

Once inside the theatre, it is doubtful that anyone, except Toffee, saw much of the film, and that young lady, having never attended a movie previously, was far too engrossed in the activities on the screen to notice anything else. To her, the gigantic reflections of racing vehicles and exploding firearms were a terribly personal matter. Mostly, she concerned herself with repeated attempts to gain the doubtful protection of Marc's lap.

The others of the party, though, were absorbed in other, more immediate problems ... most of which stemmed from the dogged efforts of a bewildered usher to seat terrorized patrons in George's seat, which indeed appeared quite vacant. On these occasions the mouthings of the screen were rudely interrupted by startled cries of surprise and subsequent accusations that usually involved Marc who was occupying the next seat. One spinsterish female, thus offended, summoned the usher and accused the cowering man of inflicting upon her unlovely person brutalities which included pinchings, proddings and other familiarities too terrible to mention. In a whisper, George vehemently denied these charges to Marc, but the die had already been cast, the usher had already threatened to call the manager if they didn't remove themselves from the premises at once.

Flushed from its retreat like a covey of reluctant quail, the party made its way silently back to the cab which was waiting in a nearby taxi stand. No one spoke to George of his misdemeanors, lest they stir in his perverse soul a rebelliousness and a will to even more awful achievements. Besides, it didn't seem that mere reprimand could possibly be enough. Apparently the taxi driver was used to being thrown out of theatres, for he seemed to find nothing untoward in this latest ejection. He seemed to take the affair of the offensive seat in his stride, too.

It was hunger that next drove the strange foursome from the semi-private confines of the taxi, and again it seemed to Marc, in retrospect, that Toffee was the one to set the project afoot.

His face a study in calamity, Marc followed his curious companions into an obscure diner with the lusterless resignation of a man who no longer gives a damn. Fully aware that the venture hadn't a Chinaman's chance for turning out well, he only hoped it would not fall into complete ruination before he at least had a chance to fortify himself with a cup of coffee.

The affair of the diner, however, all things considered, really turned out better than expected. Marc managed to choke down not just one cup of coffee, but two, before disaster came storming over the horizon. It is perfectly true, of course, that George greedily and invisibly downed a milk shake while a counter boy, three waitresses and a handful of customers looked on with goggle-eyed fascination. Even the incurious taxi driver found this phenomenon somewhat diverting. He was not entirely certain in his own mind that long distance guzzling was a standard accomplishment in the bona-fide ventriloquist's bag of tricks. In the end, he decided it probably was and looked on Marc with new respect. But there were others who gazed on the driver's new-found hero not so much with respect as disgust. Marc, for his part, pretended not to notice.

The main event, so to speak, patiently bided its time until Marc had downed the second cup of coffee. Then, on the stroke of the last drop, it commenced promptly and devastatingly. It will never be known exactly what George did to the waitress to make her so hostile, but the record definitely shows that the young woman, just passing George's stool bearing a platter of ham and eggs, suddenly jerked to a halt, turned beet red, wheeled and bestowed her messy burden squarely in Marc's face. This she followed up with a few observations on the type and dexterity of Marc's hands, which were uttered in round phrases, no cooler, in any noticeable degree, than the sizzling platter now resting on Marc's lap.

Here, the situation reached the point at which it might have taken a course for either the better or worse, pending Marc's apology to the truculent waitress. But just as Marc opened his mouth, Toffee, smitten with the injustice of it all, gave the rail switches a deft twist and sent the whole issue into a sharp decline. Lifting her water glass, in which several large cubes of ice were still afloat, she calmly and deftly reached out and poured the entire contents into the startled waitress's accommodating bodice.

It is to be supposed that a dining room brawl, at best, is bound to be an untidy business. The one that followed was hardly an exception. The employees of the diner, all accomplished hash slingers by profession, exerted every effort to prove their professional standing in a horribly literal way. What the good people lacked in cool headed aim, they made up for in sustained volume. The members of the Pillsworth party, not too ambitious, anyway, to be the victors in this war on foodstuffs, were quickly beaten into a disordered retreat. Running swiftly down the sidewalk toward the waiting taxi, their last glimpse of the enemy only caused them to redouble their efforts to be elsewhere. The counter boy and the waitresses, joined by a managerial reinforcement who had miraculously arrived on the scene in the midst of hostilities, were lined up on the sidewalk like a bespattered operatic chorus. In unison, and with gusto, they were calling for the law and horrible revenge. One of the waitresses, distinguished from the others by a spasmodic addition to quivering disturbances about the upper torso, was loudly describing the abysmal blackness of Toffee's future should she ever be permitted to arrange it.

After the skirmish in the diner, there followed a long ride in the country which might have been restful except for the persistent singing of the driver, whose favorite selection continued exasperatingly to be "Mexicali Rose." Through it all, Marc tried to assemble his thoughts, a task rather like trying to assemble a house of cards in a derailed streetcar. However, he did come to several definite conclusions. Out of the shambles that was now his life, there were two things that surely had to be salvaged. Those were his love for his wife and hers for him. Having those two ingredients with which to work he might be able to rebuild from the beginning again, providing, of course, that he did not become a permanent resident of the state penitentiary because of George's misbegotten helpfulness. Another conclusion concerned Julie's debut as a Broadway star and her certain failure as same. If Julie was to go down in humiliation, he would be there to help cushion the fall, no matter what the consequences might turn out to be.

Thus, Marc's conclusions determining their course, darkness found the taxi and its odd crew heading warily back toward the city and the Hamilton Theatre. They traveled quietly through side streets and alleys, displaying a noticeable reticence in the vicinity of bright lights and police cars. Besmirched both in character and person, the fugitives ordered their movements in concurrence with their recently lowered social status.

Marc's hope that he might be able to make his entrance into the theatre unaccompanied proved nothing more than an empty dream. The taxi driver, Toffee and the stealthy scuffling noise that was George pressed close behind him as he identified himself to the doorman backstage and went inside. Toffee had decided that the money should be carried inside the theatre for purposes of security and elected to smuggle it in under her coat. Unfortunately, with the bags stowed around her middle, the little redhead looked curiously like a very unconcerned young lady in a very delicate condition. It was an extremely unhappy arrangement.

Marc had forgotten the backstage policeman, a regular fixture in the theatre. And now that he did remember him there wasn't much that could be done about it. Standing just inside the door, the cop turned inquisitive eyes on the newcomers and started forward. As the law approached, however, the little company retreated in kind toward a shadowed area beyond several frames of scenery. They were about mid-way to this retreat when Toffee, in her haste, relaxed the hold on her coat and one of the money bags dropped to the floor with a sickening thud.

For a moment the little group stopped, transfixed in a horrified tableau, then in unison, they all became wildly animated in an attempt to retrieve the wayward pouch and return it to the place from whence it had come. By the time the policeman had drawn close enough to see what was going on, these activities were in full cry. The man of law stopped short with a startled gasp. Just why these demented people should be clutching so furiously at this woman's stomach was beyond him.

"Here, you!" he called out. "Stop that!"

The trio looked up with matching expressions of fright and guilt. All hands, except Toffee's, suddenly abandoned ship. Toffee, left to shift for herself, bent forward in a sort of agonized, doubled-up position.

The policeman drew closer for a second look, and, getting it, instantly clamped his eyes shut, his features crowding together in a look of pain. The glimpse he'd had of Toffee's mid-section had twisted his very soul. When he opened his eyes again he was careful that their gaze fell no lower than the girl's chin.

"I don't understand it, lady," he said. "What seems to be the trouble?"

Toffee flushed a deep red. "I ... I don't know, officer," she said demurely. "It just came over me all of a sudden. It's terribly embarrassing."

"I can imagine," the policeman said shortly. "If I were you, I'd be throwin' fits all over the place."

"If you were me," Toffee observed reasonably, "you'd be entitled to every fit you throw. I shouldn't think a few convulsions would go amiss, either."

This didn't rest well with the policeman and as much was registered in a disapproving scowl. "You come with me," he said sternly. "We'll find a place for you to lie down and rest a bit."

Toffee darted entreating glances to her companions, but when she received no response from either quarter, she resignedly hugged the bulging coat to her and hobbled forward in a tortured half-squat.

But the policeman didn't leave immediately. Instead, he lingered long enough to favor Marc with a long and searching glance, a glance that clearly implied an unusual interest in Marc's face. Marc didn't like the look of it. Plainly, it was the manifestation of a methodical mind that was moving methodically toward a memory that Marc feared would not be to his advantage.

All this was accomplished to a musical accompaniment that issued from the general direction of the stage. When the policeman and Toffee had gone, Marc moved quickly toward the wings.

Left with nothing else to do, the little taxi driver followed Marc, filled with the wonder of it all. It was his own impression that he had fallen in with people of true greatness. Show people. He was not concerned over the curious presence of the money bags. These folks were clearly artists given to eccentric practices in all matters ... including those of money. If they chose to carry their loose cash about in a couple of official bank sacks, why, who was he to ask questions? It was enough that they suffered him to remain in their wonderful company. The little fellow clamped the gift horse's mouth tightly shut and looked blankly in the opposite direction.

On the stage a whole regiment of very remarkable chorus girls were doggedly stomping their way through a lot of expensive scenery in pursuit of a dance routine that seemed hardly worth the effort. Marc's gaze darted beyond the girls to the other side of the stage, and his heart suddenly lifted, then shortly after, scraped against his shin on its way south of his instep. Julie, apparently awaiting a cue in the opposite wings, stared back at him wretchedly, her face too filled with fright to have room for recognition. The miracle that was needed to pull her through to success obviously hadn't come to pass.

At Marc's side, this impression was being vigorously corroborated by two diminutive bit actresses, chummily exchanging job tips to be looked into first thing in the morning.

"Too bad Linda Godfrey isn't in that dame's shoes," one of them commented sadly. "We wouldn't have to beat the pavement for the next two years."

"Yeah," the other agreed. "You know, this show was really written with Godfrey in mind. I heard the author say so himself, the other night. The poor guy was ready to hang himself when he saw La Pillsworth murdering all his best numbers."

"I hear this Pillsworth put up enough cash to steal the show from under Godfrey," the other replied. "Bet it cost him about a dozen solid gold fortunes. Money still talks, I guess."

"Too bad it doesn't sing, too. This show could use some good singing."

"Oh, I don't know. The dame's got a nice little voice when you come right down to it."

"I don't think the audience is going to get that far down, though. Anyway, that's just the trouble with her voice, it's too nice and too little. What this show needs is a big dirty voice with lots of guts. Like Godfrey's."

Marc edged away, too saddened by what he'd heard to listen to any more. Out on the stage the chorus had ceased to stalk the scenery and Julie, looking terribly alone and lonely, was moving uncertainly before the footlights. Marc felt his heart head south again as her nice little voice began to quaver over the words of a musical cynicism called "Love is a Clop in the Chops." The words of the song to the contrary, she looked and sounded like a very small girl singing in a church choir. Her lovely blondness seemed suddenly dulled and all the natural animation was drained from her blue eyes. The audience was starkly unresponsive.

Marc watched his wife's performance as long as was bearable, then turned away. He wondered how he would ever manage to say the right thing to her when it was all over. The taxi driver, however, still in the wings, seemed completely enthralled by what he saw. Marc only wished there were a thousand more of his benighted kind in the audience. Somewhere backstage a chorus girl yipped, turned about, and slapped the nearest male within reach. Apparently, George was also enjoying himself.

Marc was still deep in thought when the policeman suddenly bore down on him.

"You're Marc Pillsworth, ain't you?" the cop asked.

Marc nodded absently, and, before he thought, murmured, "Yes."

"I thought so!" the cop said triumphantly. "I was cautioned to look out for you around here. But I didn't have anything to go by except a picture in your wife's dressing room. I think the Chief might be interested in seeing you about a little bank robbery."

Marc started to back away. He'd been taken completely by surprise.

But, at that moment, Marc was not the only surprised person in the theatre. Many an eyebrow was being simultaneously hoisted out in the audience.

The chorus, having accomplished a brief change of costume, had returned to the stage, their number mysteriously increased by one. At the very end of the line a blazing redhead dressed in a seedy fur coat and a red jersey ambled calmly onto the scene, two large sacks and a wisp of filmy grey material clutched tightly in her arms. Moving quickly before a mirror that was part of the scenery, this new performer proceeded serenely about the intimate business of removing the coat and shirt, and wriggling into a light grey dress that was obstinately uncooperative. Slowly, her efforts became more and more vigorous and, from the audience's point of view, more and more exciting. This gaudy newcomer was doing a dance they hadn't seen since the days of Little Egypt, and doing it surpassingly well. In her efforts to get into the dress, she was putting her provocative anatomy through a series of gyrations and contortions that seemed beyond the limitations of mere flesh and blood. Also, to some, they seemed to outdistance the limits of ordinary decency as well.

Julie, unaware of the performance in progress behind her, misunderstood the sudden enthusiasm of the audience. She thought they had at last caught on to her subtle style of singing and were showing their appreciation. Then, turning ever so slightly, she learned, from the corner of her eye, the awful truth. At the sight of the wriggling redhead, she stopped in the middle of her song and succumbed to a tremor of rage. She didn't know who this interloper was, but she did know the stage wasn't big enough to hold the two of them. Clenching her fists, she started toward center stage and the squirming dervish in the grey dress.

A chorus girl, seeing that events were coming to a head, danced close to Toffee.

"Better put up your guard, honey," she whispered. "Here comes the star with blood in her eye."

Toffee's round eyes peered out at the girl through a chiffon fog. "What's she so upset about?" she asked innocently.

"In case you haven't heard," the girl hissed, "what you're doing is called upstaging. Honestly, you didn't think you'd get away with it, did you? In a way I'm not going to blame that Pillsworth dame when she strangles you."

"Stage!" Toffee shrieked. "Isn't this the ladies' lounge? I saw all you girls coming in here, all undressed and everything, and I...! Oh, my gosh!"

Meanwhile, backstage, Marc was too busy watching his own troubles mount to notice Toffee's predicament.

"Also, Mr. Pillsworth," the policeman was saying with maddening deliberation, "there is a certain restaurant owner that would like to have words with you. Do you want to come along quietly, or shall we mix it up a little first?"

"Oh, no," Marc moaned. "Not now, officer. Can't you put all this aside for just a bit?"

The officer shook his head and grinned nastily at the sudden flash of fear in Marc's eyes. Had he known, however, the cause of Marc's fear, he might have been less flattered by it. Behind him a steel framed folding chair was floating swiftly upward, poising itself carefully over his head.

"No!" Marc yelled. "No!"

"It's nothing to get hysterical about," the cop laughed. "We'll treat you right...."

Marc started to yell again but his words were drowned out as the wooden bottom of the chair splintered noisily over the policeman's head. A moment later the policeman tumbled to the floor, rolled over once, and then began to slither weirdly, feet first, toward the darkness beyond a nearby screen of drapes.

"No, George!" Marc yelled. "Don't drag him away! Get him some water!"

George's voice echoed back from the vicinity of the policeman's ankles. "I guess I turned up just in time, eh?"

Marc rattled off a list of words that will never be found in any dictionary. Then he started forward. It was a mistake that, in his anger, he leaped. His foot became ensnared in the wreckage of the shattered chair, and he shot head-first into space. He came down heavily against the floor, rolled partly over on his back, grinned foolishly, and lay still.

It was precisely at this moment that Julie drew abreast of the struggling redhead out on the stage.

"I'll lay you out so stiff," she grated, "people will think you're a pool cue!"

She reached out a slender, red-taloned hand and clutched a handful of grey chiffon. There was a sudden ripping sound, and then it happened. The redhead, dress and all, instantly vanished into thin air. Julie drew back with a startled cry.

The explanation of Toffee's disappearance was simple. Since she was projected into the world of reality only through Marc's full consciousness, the blow that had temporarily put an end to Marc's activities had simultaneously snuffed out Toffee's earthly existence.

To the audience, though, it was a matter of even greater simplicity. The vanishing girl was merely an excellent stage effect, excellently executed, and they applauded it with bountiful enthusiasm. They were still applauding when the curtain swung together to hide the confusion that followed.

Behind the scenes, George was briskly brushing the dust of the law from his hands as he returned to the wings where Marc still slumbered. Just why the ghost had chosen this particular moment to expend a portion of his limited ectoplasm on materialization was never quite clear; perhaps it had somehow aided him in his labors with the prostrated minion of the law. At any rate he strode, a full figure of a man, as it were, from the shadows, just as Julie emerged from the stage, the picture of pent-up rage. It was unfortunate that the paths of these two beings were fated to cross at this particular moment. Julie regarded the replica of her husband as a frost might look on a blossoming violet just prior to administering the chilly sting of death.

"You!" she seethed, unreason glowing in her eyes. "You were behind all that, Marc Pillsworth!" She gestured angrily toward the stage. "I feel it in my bones."

"I don't doubt it," George said amiably, a bit bewildered. "That dress you have on is terribly thin, isn't it?"

The barometer of Julie's control registered DANGER just before she struck George squarely on the chin. It was a blow that any professional might have been proud of. And it caused a curious sort of short-circuiting reaction in George. At the precise moment of contact, he vanished completely.

Julie stepped back, aghast. According to her tastes, this sort of thing was happening all too consistently. Then her eyes darted to Marc's hitherto unnoticed form, still crumbled some yards distant.

"Oh, my heavens!" she gasped. "I knocked him clear across the stage!"

At first she started contritely forward, then suddenly she stopped. "Serves him right," she said self-righteously.

"On stage!" a voice yelled, and Julie whirled about. A call boy was hurrying toward her. "Curtain going up on the second scene, Mrs. Pillsworth," he said. "You're supposed to be on."

Julie squared her lovely shoulders, took a deep breath, and started regally stageward. A moment later her voice rang out with a certain deadly sincerity in a song called, "I Wouldn't Give a Dime For the Ten Best Men in Town."

Meanwhile, Toffee, finding herself suddenly rematerialized, gathered up the money bags and the fur coat from a piece of scenery which was now thankfully hidden from the eyes of the audience and started in search of Marc. The redhead was now entirely clothed in the filmy grey dress that had proved the making of her theatrical success. When she found Marc he was sitting up, shaking his head. He looked at her blankly for a moment, then leaped to his feet.

"We've got to get out of here," he said. "George slugged the cop. Incidentally, where is that fiend?"

The fiend obligingly appeared, lengthwise on the floor, looking singularly unfiendish. He was a trifle fuzzy about the extremities, perhaps, but he was all there. He sat up and stroked his chin gingerly.

"Boy, that dame packs a wallop," he said unhappily.

"So justice has finally prevailed," Toffee said with satisfaction. "One of them finally nailed the right guy. And high time, too, if you ask me."

"And speaking of justice," Marc said evenly. "You have a little duty to perform, George." He removed the money bags from Toffee's arms and thrust them ungently into George's lap. "You're going to return those hellish things," he continued. "Slugging that cop was the last straw. I've had enough!"

"But I was only trying to help," George said.

Something snapped somewhere in the depths of Marc's forgiving soul. "You say that once more," he yelled, "and I'll belt you one myself!"

Hugging the bags to him, George stood up. "But the bank's closed," he said hopefully. "I can't take them back tonight."

"You'll take them back tonight, all right," Marc said with quiet intensity, "before the police find us with them. You were so smart about getting them out, now you can just dream up a way to get them back in."

The bank building loomed darkly as the taxi eased up to the curb and discharged three silent figures onto the sidewalk. Silhouetted against the glow of a distant street lamp, the figures moved forward with obvious conspiratorial intent. The first, burdened with two ominous-looking lumps of darkness, tried to hang back, and was rudely shoved forward by the other two for his efforts.

"Get those things back inside," Marc hissed, "and be snappy about it. There might be a night watchman around."

George remained unenthusiastic. "Even if I manage to fade myself through the wall," he protested, "I'll never be able to take these sacks with me. You're asking for miracles." But as Marc advanced threateningly, he started forward. "All right," he mumbled, "I'll think of something."

Marc and Toffee peered into the darkness after George as he proceeded toward the bank and finally reappeared, in silhouette again, against one of the bank's huge plate glass windows, which was dimly illuminated by a night light somewhere inside.

George seemed to hover uncertainly before the window for a time, then he bent down and seemed to take an intense interest in a trash container standing nearby. Finally he straightened up, fumbling with the bags.

"What's he doing?" Toffee asked. "He wouldn't have the nerve to pocket that money, would he?"

"I don't know," Marc replied. "He seems more to be putting something into the sacks. Rocks or something." Then he stiffened as George's motives suddenly became hideously clear. "No!" he yelled. "Don't, you fool!"

But it was too late. Already, George had swung the sacks over his head and hurled them at the window. Marc's cry rang out just as they completed their grisly mission. A horrible crashing sound was instantly followed by a loud clamor of bells, the bank's burglar alarm was heralding the awful news with a din that froze Marc and Toffee in their tracks. For one panicky moment their blood seemed to stand still in their veins.

As though by magic, the scene was suddenly filled with bounding, milling figures, most of which had a nasty, official-looking cut to them. They swarmed down on Marc and Toffee, forcing them back toward the taxi, which promptly streaked away from the curb, withdrawing its sanctuary. Apparently, the little driver had at last begun to see his new-found friends in a different light ... a prison grey, for instance. Marc and Toffee were promptly surrounded.

"We got two of 'em!" a voice yelled. "You get the other one?"

"No!" another voice answered bewilderedly. "We thought we had him but he got away somehow. Darned if I can figure out how he did it. One minute he was right here in our hands, next minute he was gone. He's a slippery rat, that one." A dull whack interrupted the voice briefly. "Ouch!" it continued. "Which one of you wise guys slugged me in the nose?"

There ensued a whole series of whacking sounds, followed by accusations, counter-accusations and athletic retaliations. Departmental jealousies and prejudices suddenly flared into the open, and the result was a sort of policemen's brawl. Later, one of the participants was heard to proclaim, whilst nursing a black eye, that he had seen a disembodied fist flying about delivering blows willy-nilly in all directions, without any noticeable favoritism to any of the various contestants. For his very accurate reportorial work, the fellow was quickly hustled off to the police psychiatrist.

George's little ruse, however, did not have the desired effect. Before the fight had effectively gotten under way, Marc and Toffee were rushed off to a police car that had screamed onto the scene with depressing promptness.

Stepping into the car, Toffee nodded toward the field of battle. "George is still helping," she observed bitterly.

"I'd like to help *him*," Marc replied dully. "I'd like to help him right through the gates of Hell."

Justice Harvey was a bear with a gavel, and he was proud because of it. With only the most delicate twist of the wrist, he could produce a resounding smack that rivaled even the awesome clatter of heavenly thunder. When the good Justice laid gavel to stand, men, women, children and morons sat up and silently searched their souls. Promptly at eleven o'clock, A.M., the Justice displayed his talent with an even greater finesse than was common. The crowded courtroom became silent, and all eyes turned hopefully to the bench.

Most of those in attendance, being either complainants or voluntary witnesses, were present in the interests in seeing a terrible justice done as speedily as possible. Many a face was alight with the fanatical gleam of vengeance.

The Justice cast a hawk-like eye toward a nearby official. "Let the crim ... the prisoner ... be brought before the bar," he proclaimed.

The official hurried importantly to a distant door and made quite a show of throwing it open. Marc, in the company of an iron-faced guard, was rudely revealed to the court, looking rather like a modest maiden lady who had been surprised in her bath. He gazed on the courtroom with an expression of embarrassment and fearful expectancy. Then he shuddered as his gaze was returned coldly by an assemblage that included the faces of such hostile personages as the bank president, the owner of the ravaged diner, the counter boy and the three waitresses. Also, among many others, there was a sprinkling of bank clerks and policemen whose features seemed not altogether unfamiliar. Marc glanced studiously at the floor as, with lagging step, he followed the official to a position of frightening prominence before the bench. A moment later, he was joined by Toffee, in the custody of a grim-looking matron.

Toffee nudged Marc. "I'm your accomplice," she said pridefully. "They say you used me for a lure."

But Marc didn't respond; he was far too fascinated by the disgusting sight of the Justice, rattling through a noisy throat-clearing operation. When it was over, the formidable servant of the public peered down at him maliciously.

"Prisoner," he thundered, "you are to be congratulated!"

"Thank you, your Honor," Marc said confusedly.

The gavel barked against the stand. "The prisoner will be silent until requested to speak," the Justice reproved. "As I was saying, you are to be congratulated. In a single day you seem to have established a criminal record that would ordinarily take a hardened thug a full year to achieve. The list of your wrongdoings is so extensive that frankly I can hardly bring myself to believe it. Virtually single-handed you have perpetrated a crime wave the like of which has not been seen in this city for the past thirty years."

"Single-handed!" Toffee snorted, injured at being relegated to a role of insulting minority. "I like that!"

The Justice fixed Toffee with a steady eye. "The court is all too well aware of your part in all this, young lady," he said. "I can only say that a girl who would allow herself to be used as a foil for innocent citizens ... who would lend her charms to the perpetra...."

"Oh, go on," Toffee broke in, pleased at having gained so much attention. "Flattery will get you almost any place with me."

The gavel performed new wonders. For a time the Justice seemed to fall into a painful lethargy. When he finally roused himself, he directed his gaze carefully at Marc.

"To continue," he said in a controlled voice, "the list of your crimes has seldom been equalled. Just for a sample, I will read off a few of the more outstanding ones. At the top of the list is a bank robbery. There is some confusion surrounding the methods used in the performance of this deed, but we are sure you will choose to explain everything at the proper time. After that, in rapid succession, there are a dozen charges of assault and battery, one of inciting to riot, two of resisting arrest, two of destruction of private property, seven of traffic violation, and one of attempted breaking and entering. The other, miscellaneous charges of improper conduct and ordinary misdemeanor seem hardly worth mentioning after all that."

This last comment provoked a brief bristling disturbance in the ranks of the complainants, most noticeable in the vicinity of the waitresses. Marc glanced toward them and quickly averted his eyes.

"Do you have a statement to make?" the Justice boomed. "Can you deny these charges?"

"Of course he can," Toffee said blandly. "He's as innocent as a newborn emu."

Toffee's careless choice of similes shocked the Justice to the extent that he forgot his resolve to ignore her. "Emu?" he asked disapprovingly. "Don't you mean a newborn babe?"

"If I'd meant babe, I'd have said babe," Toffee replied tartly. "Why should a babe be any more innocent than an emu?"

"I don't know," the Justice replied, thoroughly mixed up. "I don't even know what an emu is. A babe just seemed more appropriate, that's all."

"Just as I thought!" Toffee snapped triumphantly. "You're not fit to sit on the bench. You're prejudiced. Practically babe-crazed, too."

For one fearful second the gavel poised itself in mid-air, then it descended slowly, tremblingly to its stand, making only a faint clattering sound. The Justice's eyes roved aimlessly around the courtroom for a moment, then darted to Marc.

"Why do you let her go on like that?" he asked. "She's not making things any better for you, you know. Why don't you stop her?"

"Could you?" Marc asked hopefully.

The Justice cleared his throat and scowled. "That's neither here nor there," he said gruffly. "You were about to answer to the charges. The court wishes to know if you consider yourself guilty or not guilty."

"Will it make any difference?" Marc asked recklessly.

"Primarily," the Justice went on, "The court wishes an answer to the charge of robbery. The court knows that the money was returned in a highly informal manner, but finds no reason for leniency in this circumstance. I advise you to consider your answer carefully. The consequences will be very serious when ... if ... you are proven guilty, let me assure you. Now, answer the court with a simple statement of guilty or not guilty. It will not be necessary to elaborate."

"Not guilty," Marc said desperately. "I didn't do any of those things. It ... it was someone else."

"Someone else?" the Justice laughed nastily. "Let me tell you, Mr. Pillsworth, these infantile attempts at evasion will not avail you...."

"He is too guilty!" a voice suddenly rang out from the direction of the complainants. "He's as guilty as original sin!"

"He is not!" Toffee yelled back. She jerked back as the matron held out a restraining hand. "Get your claws off me, you lumpy old trull!"

The gavel danced a thunderous jig against its stand. "That's enough of these emotional outbursts!" the Justice hollered distractedly. "Any further demonstration, and the courtroom will be cleared." He turned a reproving eye on the matron. "Please keep the prisoner quiet," he said. "If need be, stuff a fist down her garrulous throat."

The matron nodded with a splendid show of willingness to duty. Clearly, from now on, she was only waiting her chance.

Once again the Justice turned doggedly toward Marc. "I advise you not to persist in this foolish assertion that someone other than yourself performed this list of crimes. The court is fairly jammed to the rafters with witnesses who will testify to the contrary. Can you still make such a claim in the face of all that?"

"I can," Marc said gravely. "And I do. It was someone else."

The Justice frowned impatiently. "I suppose," he said, "you are prepared to give the court a full description, if not the actual name, of this mysterious villain?"

"It was George," Toffee put in quickly.

"You shut up," the Justice said rudely, forgetting his poise.

Toffee cast the matron a murderous glance that quickly forestalled any action from that quarter. Then she turned back to the Justice. "I'm here to see that Marc gets a fair trial," she said primly.

The Justice chose to deal with Marc. "Perhaps you could tell the court what the young lady is talking about? Perhaps you can identify this George person that she alludes to?"

"Why, yes," Marc said quietly. "The young lady is right. It was George who did it all. He's a ... a...." He couldn't bring himself to say the word.

"He's lying!" The bank president was suddenly on his feet. "I saw him with my own two eyes. I don't know how he did it, but that money followed him right out the door of my bank. I'll never forget it."

The banker's cry was the spark that touched off the bonfire. Suddenly, the witnesses and complainants were on their feet in a body, crying out against Marc. Some screamed their willingness to swear in any court in the land, and promptly proved their overwhelming ability to do so in phraseology that was strikingly unlegal. Through the hub-bub, the Justice's gavel made riveting gun noises to no avail. The court had suddenly become an echoing cavern filled with a multitude of voices, all crying out for retribution. The scene was one of such hysteria that no one noticed the courtroom door sliding stealthily open and closed again, apparently of its own free will.

Before the enraged Justice, Marc began to sway slightly, all but leaning against the bench for support. He passed an unsteady hand over a forehead that was throbbing dreadfully. This was unquestionably the end. His doom was being swiftly sealed by a master craftsman called Fate, and there was nothing he could do to save himself. Worst of all, he was being taken away from Julie just at the time when she needed him most. He wondered feverishly why they didn't just lynch him and get it over with.

Even through the calamitous events of the previous day he had managed to bolster his spirits with the notion that everything would somehow clear itself up when the time came, but now he realized that he had only indulged in wishful thinking. Now, he just wanted to have done with it all. Compared to this yowling courtroom, a nice quiet cell seemed a haven of unblemished loveliness. He glanced behind him and shuddered. He seemed to be surrounded by a wall of accusing, pointing fingers.

Then he blinked and turned about. There appeared to be a curious divergence in the direction of the pointing fingers. Most of them, it was perfectly true, were pointing at him, but a few indicated a region far to the right. And even as he watched, others began to waver from him and move uncertainly away. Then, a great collective gasp scraped through the room, and was followed by a charged silence. Marc stepped forward and immediately echoed the gasp. George, fully materialized and smiling, was leaning nonchalantly against the right hand wall.

Casually smoking a cigarette, at the sight of Marc, the spirit plucked the smouldering cylinder from his lips and tossed it to the courtroom floor.

Marc's eyes promptly sought the face of the Justice. It was a grave mistake. The Justice's face, never a thing of beauty, was now an item of extreme repugnance. More than a human face, it looked like an ugly, mottled sponge that had been squeezed dry. The Justice's lips, a fierce blue color, were working at odds with each other in an attempt to say something that was probably better left unsaid.

One of the waitresses broke the spell with a shrill, hysterical giggle.

"Oh, my God!" she jabbered. "Now there's two of them!"

Justice Harvey pounded his gavel noisily as he pointed an accusing finger at George and bellowed: "How did he get into this court?"

This accurate statement of matters seemed to steady the Justice's nerves somewhat. "How ... how did you get in here, may I ask?" he demanded.

George boosted himself away from the wall and sauntered indolently toward the bar. "None of your fat-necked henchmen dragged me in," he said.

The Justice's gavel wavered uncertainly a moment, then remained at rest. The Justice regarded it dolefully. Somehow, in the last few minutes it had lost some of its appeal.

"As someone seems to have remarked," the Justice observed sadly, "we now have two of them." He sighed deeply. "Will someone volunteer to tell the court which is which?"

"It's a trick!" the bank president yelled. "We have the one that was arrested in front of my bank." He pointed to Marc. "That's the one we want!"

The crowd seemed inclined to agree. Marc, so far, had provided them with a splendid target for their injured feelings, and they were loath to give him up ... even for a replacement that was like him in every detail. Besides, this newcomer seemed the type that would fight back.

"But," the Justice put in wearily, "there appears to be a margin of doubt in this whole business ... a mighty wide margin, too. The court must be fair. A positive identification must be established." He pinched the ridge of his nose for a moment, then glanced up hopefully. "Can anyone here point to either of these men and state positively that he is the miscreant?"

"I can!"

All eyes turned to one of the waitresses as she started forward. It was the young lady who had suffered the water cure at the hands of Toffee. She placed herself stolidly before the bar, sneered briefly at Toffee, then pointed to Marc.

"That's the one," she said positively. "That silly map of his is stenciled on my memory for the rest of my life. I saw it in a nightmare last night. There's something funny about his eyes, too. No mistake, your Honor. That's the bird that did the mischief."

"You lie in your nasty bucked teeth!" Toffee rasped.

The girl whirled on Toffee, her body tense with anger. "You keep your phony two-bits worth outa this, or I'll tell his Honor what you did. I'll never be right again because of you!"

At this his Honor seemed to pick up his ears. Here was a note of intrigue worthy of his personal attention.

"What did she do?" he asked in a hushed voice.

The girl beckoned with a stained finger and the Justice obligingly leaned down over the bench. Lip-to-ear, the waitress whispered at length, and as the narrative progressed the Justice's mouth formed a scandalized O.

"All the way down?" he asked when she had finished.

The girl nodded vigorously. "And it made me feel all...."

The Justice suddenly seemed to remember that he was presiding over a court rather than a ladies' tea. His features fixed themselves into an expression of severity. "I'm not sure you should divulge confidences of such a personal nature, young lady," he said, straightening up. "However, I can see your complaint."

"Anyone can see her complaint," Toffee commented dryly. "I guess she was just born that way."

"Silence!" the Justice snapped. "And besides, this sort of thing doesn't really get us anywhere." He turned to the waitress. "You're certain this is the man, are you? No doubt in your mind whatsoever?"

"None."

"She's lying!" Toffee cried. "How *can* she be sure? They're just alike."

"Sure," George put in. "How can she be when *I'm* not so sure which of us is which. Maybe I am really he, for all I know."

"Eh?" The Justice's eyebrows seemed about to leave his face. "How's that?"

"I propose a test for the witness," George continued. "If you want a positive identification from her, why don't you let the two of us go out of the room for a moment, then return. If she can successfully pick out this gentleman over here, then we'll have to accept her testimony."

A look of deep confusion passed over the Justice's face. He turned to the waitress. "Is that a good idea?" he asked. "I'm so mixed up, I can't tell."

"Sure," the girl said. "Let 'em go. I'll pick out the right mug the minute they step through the door."

Nevertheless, something about the arrangement seemed to bother the Justice as Marc and George quickly removed themselves from the room. The minute the door closed after them, it struck him.

"Oh, my Lord!" he murmured. "Now we may never know which is which if that new one decides to double cross me. We may not even be able to tell which one was arrested outside the bank last night." He looked worriedly at the waitress. "The court's integrity is resting on you, my dear," he said.

"The court's integrity," Toffee put in, "is in one hell of a spot, in that case."

The corridor door swung open and Marc and George smilingly reappeared. Side by side, they presented themselves before the girl.

"Go ahead," the Justice urged. "Pick out the right man. Don't be nervous."

"Sure, your Honor." The girl winked broadly at her sisters-in-arms on the sidelines. "It's a cinch." She turned to the two men standing before her. Her hand went promptly toward the one on the right, and she looked back at the Justice. "That's the one, your...." Suddenly her voice faltered and trailed away into silence. She turned back to the men and her eyes darted crazily back and forth, from face to face.

"Oh, murder!" she murmured miserably. "They *are* both alike! They both even have that dirty-minded look in their eyes." For a moment she gazed up at the Justice entreatingly, and slowly began to tremble under his venomous glare. Then, all in a rush, she turned and fled to her companions from the diner. Collapsing into their out-stretched arms, she began to sob loudly.

Once more a bleak stillness gripped the courtroom. Everyone seemed to hold his breath, as though afraid not to. The only moving things in the room were the Justice's eyes, which appeared to have gone dangerously out of control. Then, after a long moment, black robed shoulders were lifted to accommodate a tremendous sigh. The gavel darted into the air and came down against the stand with a blow that split it neatly in two.

"The case is dismissed!" the justice roared. "And this damned court is adjourned!" And hurling the gavel to the floor, he lifted his robes about his ample waist and stalked ceremoniously out of the room.

Through a stunned silence, Toffee rushed gleefully to Marc and George. Reaching them, she stopped and gazed bewilderedly from one to the other, rather duplicating the performance of the remorseful waitress. Then she threw her arms around the one on the left.

"You can't fool me, Marc," she sighed happily.

Immediately, arms closed around Toffee's waist and drew her closer. She drew back.

"Let me go, George!" she cried. "You're taking advantage of my mistake."

George released her. "How did you know?" he asked disappointedly.

"Don't be silly," Toffee laughed. "If Marc ever showed that much cooperation, I'd drop dead ... of sheer joy. I'd...."

"Holy smoke!" George broke in unexpectedly. He was looking fixedly at the clock on the opposite wall.

"What's wrong?" Marc asked.

"It's only five minutes to twelve," George replied uneasily. "My thirty-six hours are all but over. The High Council will be recalling me any minute now."

Meanwhile, the spectators had joined together in a general exodus. With a definite feeling of having been cheated, they were moving toward the doorway in a sullen, grumbling tangle. Some, however, were struggling toward Marc and his companions. These were reporters.

"Oh, Judas!" Marc cried. "If you fade out right here, where they can see you, we're cooked. Let's make a run for it!"

Together, the threesome made for the only available avenue of escape ... the door to the Justice's chambers. Reaching it, they slammed it after them and turned the lock. A second later the reporters also reached it and began to pound against it. The fugitives turned to inspect their surroundings. Apparently, the Justice had already gone in search of greener, more soothing pastures, for the walnut-paneled room was deserted. They exchanged congratulatory glances and joined together in a sigh of relief.

Toffee turned to the throbbing door. "Go way!" she yelled. "We're closed for alterations!"

George's eyes, though, were on the desk clock. Now, it was only three minutes to twelve. "Tell me," the spirit said hopefully, turning to Marc, "did I really help you out there in the courtroom?"

"You were sensational, old man," Marc said, feeling a sudden warmth for the ghost. "Couldn't possibly have seen it through without you."

"You aren't just saying that to be nice, are you? The Council will have ways of knowing your true feelings."

"I wouldn't lie to you, George."

George extended his hand, and grinned as Marc accepted it. "It's been fine knowing you," he said. Then he turned away. "You know," he continued foolishly, "I feel real sentimental."

Toffee crossed to the ghost and silently took his head in her hands. "This time it's no mistake, George," she said softly. And pulling his face level with her own, she kissed him well and soundly, full on the mouth.

"What a time to be leaving," George said regretfully when it was over.

And even as he said it, he began to fade.

"Goodbye, George, old boy," Marc said. "We won't soon forget you."

"No," Toffee seconded. "Not in a million years."

George was grinning as his face dissolved into thin air. The word "goodbye" whispered through the room, and for a moment seemed to coil warmly around Marc and Toffee, engulfing them in a tide of friendliness. Then it was gone.

"You know," Toffee said thoughtfully, "he really wasn't such a bad sort. I hope he makes out well with that High Council of his. They sounded awfully heavy-handed."

"If my feelings in the matter count for anything," Marc said, "he's a cinch."

During this tender passage the drumming had continued, unnoticed, on the door. But now that George had been seen off in proper style, the insistent reporters resumed their former place of pressing immediacy on the agenda.

"We've got to get out of here before they break that door in," Marc said.

"There's a side door," Toffee observed. "The Justice must have gone out that way."

"Good night!" Marc cried. "And the darned thing has been unlocked all this time. The reporters might have walked in on us at any minute. Well, let's get out before they do."

He walked to the door and reached for the knob, but he never quite completed the motion. Suddenly, the door burst open in his face, and its edge caught him squarely between the eyes. For a moment he rocked crazily back and forth, then he closed his eyes and crumpled to the floor.

The young reporter bounded into the room and stopped short. He could have sworn he'd seen the redhead when he'd first thrown the door open, but now she didn't seem to be there at all. He searched the room systematically and finally decided the girl had only been a trick of the imagination. Settling for second best, he turned his attention to Marc.

He looked at the unconscious man and frowned. There was something odd in the way the fellow's lips kept moving. Also, something odd in his expression. He seemed to be holding a whispered conversation with someone. The reporter dropped to his knees and lowered his ear to Marc's murmuring lips.

"No, no," Marc was saying. "No, Toffee! Stop wrapping your arms around my neck like that. What are you trying to do, throttle me? Can't we say good-bye without all that?" Then he made a strange whooshing noise as though a fist had been jabbed into the pit of his stomach. For a moment his expression was angered, then it slowly relaxed. "Goodbye," he whispered. "Goodbye."

The reporter sat up, deeply perplexed. If he had been expecting to overhear an inadvertent confession, he was sadly mistaken. He wasn't quite sure just what he had heard. It didn't seem to make sense.

It might have made a great deal of sense, however, if the reporter had only known of the valley of Marc's mind and the blue mists from which Toffee had come, and to which she was returning. If the young man had only known of these things, he might easily have written the most startling story of the year. As it was, though, he only shook his head, got to his feet, and went in search of water with which to revive Marc.

It was an apprehensive Marc that left the elevator and made his way slowly toward apartment 17-B. Since the sudden departures of George and Toffee a sobering reaction had set in and certain salient facts, relative to his financial and domestic status, had made themselves hatefully apparent. That George had managed to guide the courtroom fiasco to a satisfactory conclusion hadn't really resolved any problems other than those that he, George, had created himself. Otherwise, everything was just as unsettled as before. Probably more, by now. Marc sighed heavily and proceeded to the apartment door, where his ring was quickly answered by the diminutive maid, Marie.

Marie's distress was ill concealed. "Madam is most wretched," she said. "She awakened only a bit ago, and the papers seem to have upset her terribly. I took some breakfast to her, but.... Perhaps if you went to her now...."

Marc left Marie wringing her hands in the hallway. He knocked lightly on Julie's door and when he received no answer, went on in.

Julie, looking very small and miserable against a cloud of pillows, was lavishly salting a plate of scrambled eggs with a flood of tears. She was so absorbed in this undertaking that she didn't notice Marc until he sat down beside her on the edge of the bed. Immediately, she threw her arms around his neck, buried her face against his lapel and proceeded to soak it through.

"Oh, Marc!" she sobbed. "I feel like such a horrible mess. I could die! I didn't know until I read the papers. Why didn't you tell me? I thought we were rich!"

With his free hand, Marc reached out and plucked the paper from between the pillows. The article was easy to find since it was still damp around the edges. It was the review of "Love's Gone Winging."

"Marc Pillsworth," it said, "the big advertising man from whom the Broadway wiseacres were unanimously predicting a swift and unconditional trip into the unholy state of bankruptcy, last night proved himself to be the same shrewd businessman who raised the Pillsworth Advertising Agency from a pup several years ago. With last night's opening of "Love's Gone Winging," a musical, starring none other than Mrs. Pillsworth, herself, our hero has turned out to be the sole owner of the season's most lush theatrical gold mine. He laughs best, it appears, who has the inside info on Julie Pillsworth's extraordinary talents.

"Mrs. Pillsworth, appearing courageously under her own name, has proved herself a musical comedienne of no mean standing. It is true, of course, that during her first scene she appeared nervous and restrained, but that can be attributed to first night jitters, an occupational malady that is easily forgivable on the occasion of an opening night. The real story, however, was told after the first scene. Mrs. Pillsworth, having apparently found her footing with the audience, hit the footlights with a surging vengeance that reacted on the paying customers like an electric shock. After that, she carried the show, almost single-handed, to a raging finish that had the boys and girls out front cheering the house down.

"A new dancer, a redhead unfortunately not listed on the program, appeared briefly to set the stage afire with a routine that did not dwell on inhibitions. The young lady's unusual exit was an effect that...."

The paper fell from Marc's hand and sprawled out on the floor. He could hardly believe his eyes. He gently lifted Julie's face away from his sodden lapel.

"But that's wonderful!" he said excitedly. "You were a sensation!"

"I know," Julie said dejectedly, blinking back the tears. "That's just the trouble."

"What!"

Julie nodded. "The only reason I was any good, though, was just because I was so mad I didn't know what I was doing. I haven't an ounce of talent, really. I couldn't possibly give another performance like that, even if I had to."

"Oh," Marc murmured unhappily. "Then we're washed up after all."

"Oh, no!" Julie cried. "Linda Godfrey came backstage after the show and I talked her into taking over. She knows the songs already and she's stepping into my place tonight. The show will run forever with her in it."

Wonderful relief surged through Marc. "Then why all the weeping?"

The tears welled in Julie's eyes again. "I nearly ruined you. I badgered you into it, and you let me do it, you dope. I feel awful. I feel like a fraud, too. I'm not a star. I'm just an ex-chorus girl with delusions of grandeur."

"Nonsense," Marc said. "You *are* a star. The paper says so. It's nothing to cry over, darling. Retiring like this, after a one night triumph, you'll be a Broadway legend. And on top of all that, you've steered me into one of the best investments I've ever made."

Julie blinked. Apparently she hadn't thought of it quite that way. A thoughtful smile played over her lips. "It does kind of add up that way, doesn't it?" she murmured. "Everything did turn out pretty well, didn't it?"

"Sure it did. So let's have no more of this crying. Why don't you put on your best clothes and go out and bask in your own glory, just for the thrill?"

Julie gazed up at him, and there were stars in her eyes. "You're so wonderful," she sighed. "You make everything seem so right. I wish I'd wakened you when I came in last night so we could have talked it over then. It would have saved me so much misery. But it was so late, and I felt so awful, I just didn't have the courage."

"Oh, that's all right," Marc said quickly. "Probably it was all for the...."

Suddenly he stiffened.

His gaze had wandered absently to the outspread newspaper on the floor, and a caption was shrieking up at him; "Marc Pillsworth and Unidentified Woman Jailed on Suspicion of Robbery!"

Marc's hand reached down and caught the paper in a strangle hold. Obviously, Julie hadn't bothered to look any further than the theatrical section, so, for the time being, he was still safe. He stuffed the paper under his coat and turned back to her. His throat was dry.

"Maybe you hadn't better go out after all," he said in a rush. "Maybe you'd better just stay right here, where you are. Don't get out of bed."

"What?"

"I was ... was thinking," Marc gasped. "You ... you must be awfully worn out after all those rehearsals and last night's per ... and everything. Maybe you should just stay here and rest for a few days. You know, complete rest ... no telephone calls and ... uh ... newspapers. Nothing to upset you."

Julie gazed at him questioningly for a moment, then she smiled. "Maybe you're right, dear," she said. "I do feel pretty tired at that." She reached out and patted his hand fondly. "You're so thoughtful. You do worry about me, don't you?"

Marc nodded uneasily, and gazed quickly out the window. He was feeling a little guilty.

But not very.

THE END

Milton Keynes UK
Ingram Content Group UK Ltd.
UKHW050649260624
444769UK00004B/180